This book belongs to:

For my father,
and Sue and Beccy.

Also available by Eva Eland
When Sadness Comes To Call

First published in Great Britain in 2020
by Andersen Press Ltd., 20 Vauxhall
Bridge Road, London SW1V 2SA, UK
Vijverlaan 48, 3062 HL Rotterdam, Nederland
Paperback edition first published
in 2021 by Andersen Press Ltd.
Copyright © Eva Eland 2020.
The right of Eva Eland to be
identified as the author and illustrator
of this work has been asserted by her
in accordance with the Copyright, Designs
and Patents Act, 1988.
All rights reserved. Printed and bound in the United Kingdom.
Paperback ISBN 978 1 78344 856 2
10 9 8 7 6 5 4 3 2
British Library Cataloguing in Publication Data available.
The illustrations for this book were drawn by hand then
risographed before being printed in Pantone 805U,
Pantone 102U and Pantone 299U.

Eva Eland

WHERE HAPPINESS BEGINS

Andersen Press

Are you looking for Happiness?

It often has disguises and
goes by different names.

Some days it seems to be hiding.

While on others, it's right there with you wherever you go.

You can try to
understand it,

collect it,

or protect it.

You can try to catch it...

But most
of the time
Happiness
appears to
have a will
of its own.

And sometimes it may feel as if there are too many things that get between you and Happiness.

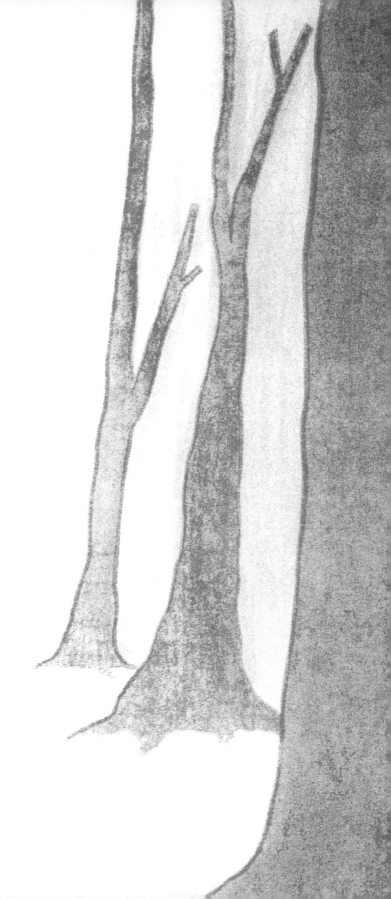

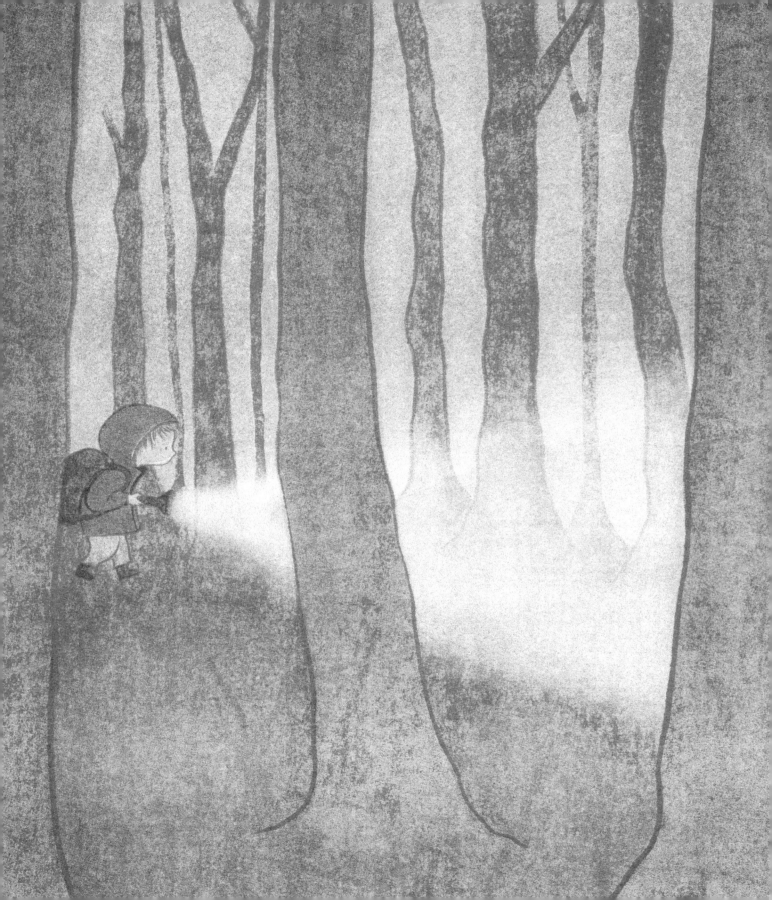

It's not always easy, but you
can find your way through

and Happiness
will be there,
waiting.

When you find it,
start following — see
where it will take you.

Happiness may be different
from what you expect, or
feel a little scary at first,

but it will let you
find new paths,
enjoy your time with
family and friends
and do the things
you love to do.

You can't feel happy all
the time. You might feel
overwhelmed by your feelings and
that you can't always control them,
but you can find your way back home.

Just breathe...

In that quiet moment
you will realise you
don't have to keep
looking for Happiness...

It was always there.
Recognise it and treasure it,
because, in the end,
Happiness begins with you.

Also by Eva Eland

WHEN
SADNESS
COMES TO CALL